SMOKE THE MOMENT

CHRIS 51

SMOKE THE MOMENT

CHRIS 51

SMOKE THE MOMENT

Copyright 2019 by Chris Rohaley, *AKA* Chris 51

All original text by Chris 51

Cover art and concept by JOSH BODWELL

ISBN 978-1-5136-5041-8
ALPHA GEEK PUBLISHING
3585 Main St.
Springfield, OR 97478
CHRIS 51
Email: Chris@chris51.com

For:

MY WIFE KATIE

And Every Smoked Moment With You

1

"Spider"
Pink Shark Club, Las Vegas
★ 1986 ★

"You gotta take your hat off, buddy," demanded the gargantuan Samoan doorman with a less than enthusiastic expression on his tan face. The enormous bouncer was practically ripping out of his tight, pink staff shirt that made him look like an oversized Easter Peep on steroids. He could belittle any man with nothing but a neutral stare.

"Hey, no problem," returned Spider as he ripped his hat off and folded it into his back pocket. Spider was greeted by two more wooly mammoth men who opened the club's giant steel doors to let him in. The Pink Shark was currently the hottest nightclub in Vegas, and with the line of girls in miniskirts and Aqua-Net updos waiting to get in, he wasn't going to ruin his chances to score by wearing a stupid pompadour.

With his first step inside the Shark's mouth, a devilish choir sang seductive songs of lust and opportunity in his head.

Spider knew that tonight was going to be unforgettable. The intro to Falco's "Rock Me Amadeus" synced perfectly to his first steps through the jagged, steel-arched entry, like a setup for an MTV video montage.

A giant aquarium was affixed atop the bar to his right, but the pair of swirling sharks inside weren't half as impressive as the curvy go-go dancers in pink G-string bikinis beside them. These girls were a dime; a perfect ten that consisted of nine parts fake tits, tans, and blonde hair, and one part of who gave a shit else. They twirled around like veteran strippers not yet worn out by hard times and old dick and climbed on the life-preserver-ringed brass poles that attached each corner of the bar to the twenty-foot-high ceiling. If Vegas had become a cocaine and sex-infested playground for twenty-somethings, this club was the epicenter of powder and sin.

Spider loved Vegas. He felt like his life was a Hollywood movie, and he narrated it daily with fun and indifference. He punctuated each day's story with a quest for a different girl, and if he couldn't fill his nights with pussy, he would climax with the best drugs this side of Columbia! The neon lights fueled the party, and like the city's slogan, Spider never slept.

With martini in hand, Spider quickly warmed up to the perfect ensemble of groupies who looked like they came straight from a Madonna video, complete with fishnet arm sleeves, the minniest of miniskirts, and giant, sparkling gold hoop earrings. As the groupies found their seats in the rear of the club by the huge, plastic, pink palm trees, Spider innocently removed his pompadour from his back pocket and replaced it atop his slicked jet-black hair, forgetting the Neanderthal bouncer's previous warning. He was trapped in a trance of perfume and arousal and guided by the head in his pants, not the one on his shoulders.

Just as he punctuated a phrase that would seal the one-night deal with an intoxicated, infatuated girl, a hand swatted the back of his head and knocked his pompadour off so violently that it landed on the table in front of him, knocking over all the drinks like a row of expensive martini dominos.

"I thought I told you no hats, you fuckin' Guido." The abominable marshmallow Peep-shaped doorman, with a clan of two other Sasquatch-sized Samoan bouncers, had already flanked Spider, as if they were just waiting in a racist-inspired stakeout to sabotage his night.

With an immediate smirk of overconfidence, Spider leaned over and grabbed the only martini left standing on the alcohol-flooded table. He plucked a lonely olive that was floating in the expensive puddle and popped it in his mouth, followed by one giant swallow that finished off the entire cocktail. He gently set the glass down, his back still to the bouncer. Slowly, he turned around, deliberately taking his sweet time.

"Fuck you, you fat piece of shit," probably wasn't the wisest rebuttal, but Spider had to keep his game face on. He had pussy on the line, but more importantly, he had his pride. *Nobody pushes around this Italian in this town,* he thought, as his drug-induced "everybody wants some" attitude squandered his rationality. But before his pointed finger could bull's-eye the doorman's chest, all three giants had all six hands on Spider's torso.

Kicking and cussing the whole way, Spider did not go out

in a gentle web of cooperation and ease. Other than a few scratches to the security's impenetrable Island skin and a bruised ego or two, Spider was removed from the premises with little group effort. After they threw him on the parking lot asphalt into an oil-ringed puddle, Spider jumped up quickly and exacted his only means of revenge by forcing one hell of a spitwad toward the doorman's head. The snot-infused saliva literally exploded upon impact and nearly blanketed the Samoan's entire face.

Within an instant all three Samoans followed their counterparts' lead in attacking Spider on the ground. The beatdown was not subtle, and the violent commotion interrupted the lineup of girls outside the club. Like an overflowing anthill, the women poured around the glass barrier in droves to witness the brutal assault in the parking lot beside the Pink Shark.

The crackling sound of broken ribs worsened as the gang repeatedly kicked in the sides of the defenseless Italian. As Spider frantically tried to crawl away, the doorman implemented a last display of pride. Like the ancient Samoan custom of punishment, the aggressor pulled a bamboo switch from his boot and began whipping Spider's calves. A tradition of torture passed down generations, this beating would cripple Spider's walking performance for months to come.

With his clean, white Firebird only four parking spaces away from where he now lay abused and bloodied, Spider was finally free to crawl to his car. He pulled himself up to the handle and unlatched the door, leaving a bloody handprint on his newly washed paintjob. With adrenaline overpowering his pain receptors, he managed to stand up and reach for his gun from behind the seat.

Spider turned around with enough time to catch the security detail still walking into the club's rear door. "You fat motherfuckers!" he yelled as he unloaded round after round of a 9 mm chrome pistol. With the whipping motion of the gun, he struck the glass barrier separating the club entry and the side lot several times, drenching the slutty bystanders in a hail of glass shards. A shot connected with the rear bouncer entering the club, and he fell to the floor in the door way, leaving it pried open with his giant, bloodied body.

Screams of terror permeated the sticky night air in Vegas. Attendants fled the front doors by the dozens as Spider limped toward the steel doors.

The downed bouncer managed to get up on his knees and crawled behind the open door before Spider caught up to him. The bouncer grabbed the first weapon available, a bat the staff kept in a nook behind the door jam. When Spider walked through the door, a surprise homerun swing did little extra damage to his already shattered ribs, and he recovered quickly to unload a shot on the bouncer. The Samoan immediately slumped to the floor, dropping the Louisville Slugger. Spider watched as it rolled away on a trajectory, like a compass pointing right to his next target.

The second guard was scurrying away like a fat hippo up a muddy hill on the stairs to the second level. Spider pulled off a couple more wild blasts and managed to catch him at the top. He fell down the pink carpeted staircase, turning them a dark red as he tumbled to a sudden splash at Spider's feet. Spider stepped over the large hump of shit without missing a beat, his eyes completely fixated on the path before him.

On the second floor Spider started shooting aimlessly at closed doors, determined to wipe out his final offender. As he neared the end of the hall, he heard a rustling behind him. The doorman, and last man standing, scuttled from behind a velvet couch toward the stairs, remembering that there was gun was down there behind the bar. Spider raised his weapon and effortlessly squeezed off a single shot. The bullet clipped the doorman's Achilles tendon, sending him flying down the stairs, landing in the bloody pile that once was his coworker. The Samoan managed to get up and turned around to face his aggressor. Spider reached the final few stairs and fired one, two, three shots from his spider engraved gun into the fat man's pink shirt without even looking him in the eye, all while walking right past him toward the exit. He swung open the front doors and limped out to the sound of sirens.

2

"Circling Sharks"
Dirty Alley
★ 1987 ★

Spider leaned back and settled into an old, dirty, gold couch in an alley behind one of the antiquated giant casinos in old town. He recounted the incident with pride.

"No fuckin' way, dude. That was you," gushed Ricky. "You are a legend around here, man. I totally remember that last year. Didn't they call it the Pink Shark Slaughter?"

"Yeah, although it wasn't really a slaughter cause I only killed three fools," said Spider, sounding almost disappointed. "But you gotta smoke the moment."

"Smoke the moment, I like that." Ricky bounced back. "Well then how are you even here . . . why aren't you doin' life, man?" Ricky tried to get relaxed on the couch too, but the energy of Spider's story had him on the edge of the stained cushion.

"Well like thirty girls that were outside the club testified about how bad those dudes were beatin' on me. I got off with temporary insanity."

"That is a crazy fuckin story, man. Wow!" Ricky shook his head and threw his hands up. "How the fuck did you get out of that one?"

"I know, right?" Spider was practically bragging. "I definitely wasn't temporarily insane or whatever, I knew exactly what I was doing the whole time. I wanted to kill those fat bastards!"

"No shit? Well, remind me to never piss you off," joked Ricky. "Well, let's try this shit." Ricky secretly questioned Spider's mental stability now and started fidgeting.

"You take the first hit," said Spider as he handed Ricky the pipe. He chuckled. "Remember, you gotta smoke the moment!"

"Ohh my God, this shit is totally rad," Ricky muttered in a smoke-filled breath. "Now I am really glad I met you." As the two began their drug-seduced friendship, the trance of the meth quickly overpowered any doubt of Spider's sanity in Ricky's mind.

The two had met just a few weeks earlier through a dealer in the Golden Nugget bathroom. They hit it off immediately, sharing the same tastes in all the cheap and exotic intoxicants that the dirty underbelly of Vegas had to offer. They had been living high and growing close, pulling off small-time cons, purse snatches, and pickpockets together to keep their roller-coaster high ride on the track. They were a deviant duo, and they were good at what they did.

Spider had been barely eking through life since his legal

battles, and reputation preceded him in every endeavor he attempted. Even when he tried to straighten up his life, trouble and temptation always easily found him, and it didn't take much self-justification to quit when things got hard. It wasn't the murder and inner demons that Spider struggled with—it was the feeling that he was cheated out of his future, and the clinging to the axiom that life was unfair. He never thought twice about the killings, only the repercussions that those fuckin Samoans had cost him.

Ricky, on the other hand, was a victim of self-induced idiotic choices and weak mindedness. When he was sober, he was cheating on partners or leaving a trail of deceit in relationship wakes. When he was single, he could never handle sobriety. He was in a constant emotional battle to better himself but didn't have the courage to face life's challenges alone. Ricky never had the fortitude to take life by the balls and always hid behind a volcano of excuses and blame.

Together, they fed off of each other's failures and shortcomings, blaming society for their problems and fueling their passion for just enjoying the rest of the ride by escaping reality.

3

"Cinnamon"

Las Vegas Suburbs
★ 1988 ★

Across town, above an old record store, were a few dingy apartments. The building was rotting away at its concrete core, but the dozen layers of flat, black paint and thousands of band stickers somehow held it together. It was a local hangout for headbangers and glam rockers, often providing a parking lot battlefield for Mötley Crüevians vs. Depeche Modians. There was never any shortage of sluts or drugs being shared around the local clientele.

Unbeknownst to anyone, one of the apartments was completely thrashed. Cupboards had been emptied to a pile of shattered dishes on the kitchen floor. Overturned couch cushions and a broken coffee table centered a living room full of thrown-about jewelry boxes, slutty stripper paraphernalia, and knocked-over lamps. There was an empty oak cabinet with a dust ring where a TV and VCR used to sit. A shattered framed poster of Duran Duran punctuated the pile of new-wave chaos.

Iron Maiden's "Wasted Years" played from below, muffling the sound of keys jiggling outside the apartment door. The door gently creaked open like the sound of a cheesy horror-movie killer's entrance. The keys suddenly dropped next to a pair of sexy painted toes adorning some expensive red high heels. Then a grocery bag fell next to them, and a lonely orange rolled to the center of the devastation that lay before her.

Cinnamon couldn't believe her own eyes. Everything she'd worked so hard for over the last six months, trying to make her own way, was gone or destroyed. All the lap dances on fat, sweaty Mexicans, and the Italians ramming their pinkies up her butthole, all now for nothing. All the nasty boners she had rubbed against without ever feeling one that she actually wanted to be waiting at home, now all a fucking waste of time and tolerance. All the promises she'd made her mom, and only months away from fulfilling them and going back to school, now would be nothing more than fairy tales.

She ran into her room to check the unicorn. It was an old cookie jar she adored from her childhood in Oregon. It was a remembrance of simpler times. It was motivation to make something of herself. It was full of all her savings to get out of this filthy life. It was . . . smashed to a thousand pieces on the floor. The unicorn was empty. Cinnamon was empty.

"Becca's Call"
Another Dirty Alley-Las Vegas
★ 1987 ★

Ricky was slumped over a puddle of his own vomit in an alley. Or was it someone else's? He didn't know—or even really care. He wondered if he'd ever even left the alley after scoring his fix the previous afternoon. Or was it the previous morning? *What time is it now, 2:00, 3:00?* He speculated as he reached in his pocket for his pager. 9:11, *shit it is early, or wait . . . that says 911, not 9:11.*

"What the fuck?" he questioned out loud. He laid his head back against the molded cinder block wall that already left a nice residue of peeled paint in his thinning hair from his previous siesta. Just as he was about to convince himself that whoever was paging him could wait, he realized that the number's area code might be familiar. 239, 239. *Ohh shit, that is Florida, that's home! That's real life.* That, is the only important thing worth getting up for. Ricky grabbed at anything he could as he attempted to get vertical. He used the wall for balance, and it took some effort to get up on his feet. With every step he took out of the alley's mouth, he used the wall a little less as a crutch and a little more as a landmark of where he might actually be. At this point he didn't really care about where he was, though, just where a pay phone was.

"Hello," answered a shaky voice on the receiving end. It sounded panicked.

"Becca, it's Ricky. What's going on?" His greasy head pressed against the inside of the phone booth glass to help him stand upright.

"Ohh my God, Ricky, its Ashley, she's sick!" Becca was frantic.

"What?" A shot of fear and adrenaline immediately straightened Ricky's posture and balance. "What do you mean 'sick'?"

"She had constant pain, so I took her in to get examined. The doctor just told me she has a rare liver disease. Her doctor said she needs a transplant soon, or she could die. I just don't know what to do, I just . . ." Becca abruptly halted to uncontrollable crying.

"What? Why didn't you tell me all this was going on? I would have come there right away. Holy shit, what should I do?'"

"I didn't tell you because you are always fuckin high whenever I call you, and I don't want her to see you like that. The only reason I am even telling you now is because Ashley keeps asking for you. She wants to see you, and she really needs you. I don't know why or even think you deserve it, but I am not going to deprive my sick child of anything at this moment. Court order aside, I want you here with her."

"As of right now I am not high anymore. I promise! I want to see her." *She is the only part of me that is good; nothing can happen to her, or I will have nothing worth living for,* Ricky thought. He was holding back a complete mental breakdown. He knew that for once in his life he had to be strong for them all, or Becca would never make it through this, and if she didn't, his daughter wouldn't either.

Ricky never treated Becca too well, always looking over his shoulder for the next better thing. Whether that next rush was from drugs or women, his relationship with her was buried long ago. But this was different. For this he would put aside any old problems or feelings.

"Ricky, the doctor can't even put her on the donor waiting list without a deposit, and I don't have insurance. They need $8,000 just to get started. I sold my car, but . . ."

"Don't worry, Becca, I will find a way. Whatever the fuck I have to do, I will find a way. I will get the money!"

"You better, Ricky! You better do the right thing for once in your life. When can you get here? She wants to see you."

"I am on my way." Ricky slammed the phone down, took a huge deep breath, and completely firmed up, like Frankenstein's monster just brought to life. He grabbed the backpack at his feet, which held everything he currently owned in the world, and slung it over his shoulder. He dusted off his pants and ran his dirty fingers through his even dirtier hair. He pulled his Van Halen tour T-shirt up to his face to wipe off a layer of oil in a half-assed attempt to feel somewhat presentable. Ricky instantly sobered up, and for the first time in a long time, the thought of getting high was the furthest thing from his mind.

He had needed a reason to get back on his feet after days of struggling to leave the delirious comfort of that grimy alley. He bolted out fueled by a newfound motivation. His daughter was the one thing in the world that might just catapult him from his downward spiral.

Ricky walked across the street toward the freeway entrance and stuck out his thumb. Without bus fare this would be a difficult journey, especially while simultaneously detoxing, but Ricky was focused for the first time in what seemed like a lifetime. There was no stopping him now. He would walk the entire way if he had to.

5

"The Stage"

Cinnamon is Back at Work
★ 1988 ★

"Gentlemen, please welcome to the main stage, the one and only queen of spice and lace, the sexy redhead all hot in red . . . Cinnnnnnaaaamon!" The voice blared over the club's loudspeaker in the most cliché douchebag-titty-bar announcer voice possible. She slowly stepped out from behind the velvet curtain matching every footstep to the beat of Duran Duran's "The Reflex." Cinnamon's face was covered with her thick, fiery hair as she seductively approached the brass pole in six-inch stilettos. She raised her arms above her heart to release a red-feathered boa balancing on her shoulders. As it floated to the floor behind her, Cinnamon whipped her head back to release the hair from her face and jumped on the pole all in one smooth choreographed motion.

She hated the name Cinnamon. But she didn't have much choice in the matter. The manager gave each girl a name when they were hired, whether they liked it or not. It was part of the business, she got that, but it still made her skin crawl every time she heard it on that loudspeaker.

"Ouuuuuuuie!" blurted an obnoxious patron sitting at the brass rail. "Crawl your fine ass over here, honey. I got some cash with your name all over it!"

With no other options on such a slow night, Cinnamon had little choice but to follow the slimy pervert's instructions if she was to afford groceries the next day. She finished her twirl on the pole and landed perfectly on her red heals. She then turned her back toward the crowd, revealing the most perfect round ass known to man, covered only by a thin red G-string with a red star that connected the cross string. She reached one arm up her back and unsnapped her delicate lace bra with the grace of a petite ballerina, like she had a hundred times before.

She spun back toward the allure of the cash with arms folded across her chest. One by one, she slowly removed each arm to reveal her hot pink glowing nipples on her small but rock-hard perky breasts. She knelt down to the stage floor and began a cat-like crawl toward the raunchy customer, dreading each movement more than the last, but hiding the pain like a pro.

When she reached him, the light revealed the face that had been hiding under his snakeskin cowboy hat.

"Hey, Cinnamon darling," spoke the voice under the brim.

"Hi, Spider," Cinnamon whispered with camouflaged disgust. "It's been a while."

She couldn't stand Spider, a longtime regular at the club who had been MIA for a few months. He always wanted only her, and his hands always grabbed way too much. All he ever did was brag to her about how cool and badass he was, like he was trying to convince himself. Every lap dance was the same conversation, and after every song her answer was no to his advances, typically followed by a slap across Spider's face.

But this time he seemed different. There was a serious, more focused look on his face. Spider leaned in close to her neck.

"Listen, honey, I got a job for you."

"Sure, Spider, where have I heard that before. You know I don't do that."

"No, no, no. Not a blow job, a business proposition, with real money. Lots of money. Enough to get you off of this stage for good. I know you want that," explained Spider in the most serious connotation.

"Not interested," Cinnamon rebounded without skipping a beat.

"Just hear me out, darling. Listen, I'll pay you for a lap dance and you don't even have to get naked or touch me. Can we just go somewhere private to talk?"

Now this was a first. Cinnamon had never heard anything like this from Spider. Something was definitely different and almost . . . sincere. Spider was always just about groping her body or making crude sexual advances, never any real conversation or any talk with a hint of substance. In fact, she tried recalling if Spider ever really made actual eye contact while talking to her before. For the first time ever, he was completely sober.

"I guess, but I swear to God if you try anything, Spider, I

will have you eighty-sixed from here for life. I'm not taking your shit anymore."

Mentally, Cinnamon was a much stronger woman now than when Spider visited her on the regular months ago. After her robbery, she had hardened and refused to be a victim anymore. Her pale ginger skin had definitely gotten thicker and her attitude was less passive.

She rubbed her tits in Spider's face to keep appearances and stood back up. She walked across stage to a new customer who had eagerly lined up a few dollar bills on the rail. She knelt down again, pulled the fat Asian close by his tie, and blew in his ear. A childlike smile came over his face, and he seemed to be satisfied. It was all she could muster, as her mind was now so preoccupied on Spider's offer. *What in the world could it be,* she thought. Was it really on the up and up? Could it really get her out of this place she's tried so hard to leave before? Could it be enough for her to start school? She shoved the guy back to his seat and he giggled. Swooping up the dollars, Cinnamon rose to her feet and walked off stage just as "Girls, Girls, Girls" gave way to "Like a Virgin."

Now in a cherry-red skintight minidress, with her hard nipples daring to poke holes through the material, Cinnamon walked around from behind the stage toward Spider. With the club's rotating spotlights now focused on a huge-breasted blonde on the main stage, Cinnamon was free to have a more private discussion with Spider. She grabbed for his hand and he gently took it. Just from his gentle touch, she knew something was extremely different with him. His hand wasn't sweaty and clingy; he was all business. They turned, and she led them toward the private VIP room.

21

"Another Different Alley"
Fort Myers, Florida
★ 1988 ★

How did I get back here, Ricky thought. Another piss-laden dark alley hiding behind another filthy dumpster, searching for solutions behind a Kwik-E-Mart. But this time was different; this time he was in control of his mind and his habits. And yet the same could not be said of his heart, which was very much in control of everything else.

He couldn't afford rehab and had no insurance of any kind, so he had to overcome the torturous weeks of withdrawals all on his own. The love and impending death of a child is a powerful motivator. The vomiting and migraines were hellacious, but nothing compared to the mental anguish over his little girl. He was clean and sober but hurting so badly inside; not from the lifetime abuse of drugs rotting his organs, but from thoughts of his daughter getting sicker by the day. Even with all the honest odd jobs he'd worked over the last few months, and all the sweat and lack of sleep, he still had nowhere near the money he needed to help her. He was desperate.

Ricky stood quietly in the shadow of his enormous doubt, waiting for the opportune moment. Little did he know when he left Vegas months prior that he would need to use the one thing he swore he never would again. At this moment, and for this reason only, he was glad he kept his gun. He rechecked the chamber for the third time to confirm it was still empty. He put the gun in his front hoodie pocket barrel first, took a deep breath, and stepped out from behind the rusted trash bin. His heart was racing faster than it had ever felt from any drug. He knew his whole life could change in the blink of an eye, but he didn't care. All he could think about was those big, brown seven-year old eyes making his heart beat.

Suddenly, his feet stopped moving before his brain even sent them the command. The register in the Kwik-E-Mart was less than thirty feet away, but he couldn't take another step toward it. A middle-aged man and a little girl entered the convenience store holding hands. She was skipping and humming, using his steady hand for balance. *A father and daughter! What the fuck am I doing?* Ricky thought to himself with disgust and sadness. *I can't do this; what if something went wrong? What if that little girl got hurt? I would be putting them in the same position that I am in right now.* Ricky grabbed his hair with his hands as if he were going to pull out every last strand. He wanted to scream aloud, but managed to let the anguish slip out internally.

"I can't do this," he murmured. "Fuck this, I'll find another way."

Ricky turned back into the alley and threw his gun into the old dumpster. *I don't ever want to be tempted to use this thing again!*

Ricky looked to the sky almost to ask why, and just let the sun beat down on his face for a minute. His feet would not yet allow him to move forward. He stood in front of the alley for several minutes just pondering his choices and wondering why he never had a single moment of good luck or fortune in his entire life. *Just one break,* he thought to himself. *Can't I just get one lucky break for once in my life,* he questioned the sky above.

When the sun finally baked him back to reality, Ricky checked his watch and realized he better get his ass working so he wouldn't lose out on the only thing that was helping him save his daughter, however miniscule. He lowered his head and walked away in defeat once again.

7

"The Job Offer"
Fort Myers, Florida
★ 1988 ★

"Ricky, what's goin on my man, it's Spider. How's Florida treatin' ya?"

"Hey, dude, good to hear from you. Sucks down here, man. No fuckin' work . . . my daughter is getting worse . . . it is hot as fuck." Ricky sat inside the sauna of a phone booth. Although a cold chill had come across his skin when he'd seen a Vegas number on his beeper, it had quickly turned to sweaty dread when he discovered it was Spider on the receiving end.

"Well then, my timing is perfect—as usual," boasted Spider in his typical cocky tone. "Boy, have I got a job for you!" Ricky cringed. Spider's "jobs'" were never of the legal or moral variety, and Ricky's sweat from the hot phone box immediately doubled with sweat from anxiety.

"I can't, dude, I have way too much going on down here with my daughter and all. That is all I care about now." There was no way Ricky was gonna get involved in that old life that he'd been trying so hard to move past.

"You haven't even let me tell you what it is," Spider rebutted.

"I don't care, man. I am clean now and I am where I need to be."

"Would $20,000 change your mind?"

Silence filled the phone receiver for a few seconds as Ricky leaned his head against the booth's glass. He took a deep breath. This could get Ashley on the transplant waiting list, and maybe even the surgery. Was he actually considering listening to Spider? Did he trust that slick Italian for one second? No. But, did he have no choice but to hear him out? Yes.

"Did you hear me, Ricky?"

"What do I gotta do?" Ricky raised his head from the glass and gave it a quick shake to regain his composure.

"I don't want to say over the phone, but you have to trust me. Just get back here before Christmas Eve. I need you for only a couple days, then the money is yours. Easy work, man," Spider offered.

"I am leaving for the bus station right now." He had to take this huge risk and trust his old friend. Why before Christmas Eve, and why now when he needed it most? This would be a test of his faith and fortitude on every possible level.

It wasn't going to be easy to leave Ashley yet again, even if for the right reasons this time. Just a few weeks earlier he'd finally felt they really reconnected, and she'd let go of any last resentment toward him. They were at the beach, eating ice cream on the pier. As Ricky was telling Ashley what species of fish the anglers were pulling up, she'd tripped on a lifted section of plank, and her ice cream cone went flying over the edge. They'd both peered over to see its final demise but discovered it had landed on a support beam that protruded from under the walkway. To Ashley's amazement, and her dad's insistence that she not do it, Ricky had saved the day by climbing over the railing to fetch the cone that was still intact. He had reacted without hesitation. He'd climbed back up over the railing with trophy in hand and swept off the dirty portion of cream to preserve the best part of the waffle cone for his girl.

Little Ashley had Alagille syndrome, a rare disorder that affects small children and in her case would certainly be fatal without a transplant. Without steady work and zero possibility for health insurance, there was no way Ashley could even be added to a transplant donor list. As a part-time waitress at Perkins, Becca certainly couldn't help, and somehow Ricky felt responsible because of his lifelong drug abuse. It had to have a factor in Ashley's health.

Their last doctor's visit didn't go so well. Ricky took Ashley to the checkup alone since Becca had to work. It was the first time she trusted him with this responsibility. However, he didn't have the heart to tell Becca the real outcome of the examination. The sickness was progressing faster than anticipated, and the window for remedy was rapidly closing.

If he wanted his daughter to live, he would have to face his demons one last time. With all of society's normal options for employment exhausted, it was time to do whatever it took to amend the evils in his own life.

"Cinnamon Takes Flight"
Kenosha, Wisconsin
★ 1986 ★

She had been so excited to answer that call from Pan Am Airlines. She put the phone down and shrieked with excitement. She thought being a stewardess was going to change her life. She was going to see the world.

She didn't know what she wanted to be in life; she just knew she wanted out of her current one. There was no future in Kenosha unless it involved bartending to old, drunk perverts, catfishing, or hunting from a tree stand in the cold-as-fuck winter. She didn't want any of it. She didn't want to end up pregnant by eighteen or nineteen like all her friends' older siblings. All that there was to do there was drink and fuck, and she didn't really care for either.

Her parents worked hard, but couldn't afford to help her go to college. It was hard enough keeping their cows from freezing in the winter, let alone keeping the heat on in the house. Dad tended to the fields and livestock all day while Mom made quilts to sell during her downtime from cooking and cleaning after four messy boys and of course, one little redhead girl.

If the boys were lucky, they at least had a chance. If they were good enough at football or baseball, they might get a ticket out of town and an opportunity to become something more than future poor farmers. Although, most who did get out eventually ended up coming back to do just that.

The second she'd turned seventeen she applied for Pan Am. For her, it was the most luxurious job she could ever get without going to college. It was like experiencing a new life with every flight. It took a couple tries, but by the summer after high school, she got the call.

Her dad had driven her to the Minneapolis airport. It was the first time she'd ever seen him cry. He'd given her $120 which he'd probably been saving for a year. It was everything he had.

"Don't tell your brothers, Firecracker." He had called her that because of her temper when she was younger, and her red hair, of course. She'd always loved that name.

"You be careful. Boys out there ain't like boys here, they are evil men. Lots of Devils in in the shadows of those big cities." At the time, she'd thought he was just being overprotective. "You come home whenever you want, you always have a place here."

So far, she had been to over ten cities. She had seen a couple museums and national landmarks. She made the most of her little free time between flights. She had been in the St.

Louis Arch and on Alcatraz Island. She swam in both the Atlantic and Pacific. In just a month, she had done and seen more than all her girlfriends would in their entire life time. She was living the dream. But nothing compared to her next trip—Las Vegas! She was excited for this one above all others. The city of lights, the city of fortune, the city of sin . . .

"Bogey"
Las Vegas
★ 1988 ★

In a very large house, in an unassuming, affluent neighborhood in North Vegas, an extremely large black man carried a ringing phone. He picked up the receiver and put it against the ear of a much skinnier black man running on a treadmill. The runner didn't bother stopping; no call at this point in time would seem important enough to do so. The treadmill was facing the street, behind a very tall wall of cascading windows, so the runner had a great peripheral view of the neighborhood and approaching cars.

"Yo?"

"Bogey?" Ricky should have been paranoid to make this call, and in the past, he would have been, but dire circumstances make for a more confident man.

"Yeah, who dis?" Bogey didn't miss a step or a breath.

"Dude, it's Ricky."

"Holy shit, Sticky Ricky! What's up my negro from a honky amigo?" Bogey jumped off the treadmill. Ricky's voice was enough of a surprise for Bogey to stop and actually focus on the call, which he rarely did.

"Lots man, lots of shit. I'm totally clean now and living in Florida, but I need a quick job if you know what I mean. I have an emergency with home life," Ricky explained. "I'll be back in town real soon and I need a little insurance."

"Florida, shit, man. That's cool, you know you are always my nigga. I got just the thing for you. Come see me when you get to town," Bogey offered. Bogey hadn't seen or heard from Ricky in a long time, but he knew that Ricky was always trustworthy and reliable. If the price or fix was right, he would get any job done. But it had been some time. If Ricky was calling him now, he knew he must be desperate, and Bogey could use that to his own advantage.

"Thanks, man, I appreciate it. See you in a couple days."

"Cool, my brother, see you then," finished Bogey.

Doing jobs for Bogey meant owing Bogey, and it also opened the door to lots of drugs, which was exactly the torture Ricky didn't want to be faced with but knew Bogey could always control him with. Bogey's feel-good rewards were what got Ricky hooked in the first place. And Bogey would expect payback for the opportunities he provided, that were much bigger than the original job to begin with. In short, working for Bogey meant Bogey owned your ass.

A couple years back Bogey got wind of Ricky's purse- and wallet-snatching escapades on a section of turf that he ran. Nothing happened north of Old Town without Bogey knowing about it or getting a piece of it. Bogey had his guys catch this deviant and bring him to the house for a polite ultimatum. Ricky was given a simple choice: continue with the pickpocketing and snatching that he was so talented at and split the proceeds with Bogey, or be split in two and left in the desert for the crows to pick at. Ricky obeyed so well that he quickly rose up the ranks of Bogey's more reliable degenerates.

Bogey was a master of all petty to moderate criminal trades. He hocked cars, stole deliveries, conned tourists, and dealt drugs. He had several minions around Vegas to do his ungodly deeds, so he never had to get his hands dirty. Bogey's deeds put a lot of dudes behind bars but alternatively made a lot of guys money.

He always wore wifebeaters with thick gold chains and the most stylish and expensive Adidas shoes. He was so skinny, in fact, that you'd swear he personally tested all the crack he sold, but in reality, he was just a treadmill junkie. He was always on the treadmill; for every deal and phone call, meeting and handshake, he lived on that treadmill. He didn't even sweat or care to be fit; he just didn't like to leave his house and couldn't sit still. In truth, he probably didn't leave the house because he made so many enemies around town and pissed off all the wrong people. He was paranoid and anxious, which is also why he couldn't sit still.

Ricky was one of Bogey's star con men for years. He had wondered what happened to him from time to time. Bogey just assumed that he overdosed in an alley somewhere because of the way the drugs took control of his life . . . and he wouldn't have been far off if not for that one phone call Ricky got.

Bogey always liked Ricky, and even held a small level of respect for him since he got any job done, no matter how fucked up he was. He never squealed and never came back empty-handed with excuses. Ricky was weak and easy to manipulate. Bogey, on the other hand, was not.

"Ricky's Back in Town"
Las Vegas
★ 1988 ★

As soon as the dust-coated Greyhound pulled into the Vegas station, Ricky noticed the all-too-familiar car. A white Firebird with a custom Spider airbrushed on the hood that would put Smokey's bandit to shame. The T-top was open to reveal the red leather interior, and from the bus, he could see the chrome steering wheel with a shining tarantula engraving. Leaning against the trunk wearing his snakeskin cowboy hat and boots and giant, silver spider-shaped belt buckle was his old partner in crime. Ricky was used to the obnoxious car, and he could even deal with the stupid hat, but the belt buckle was just too over the top, even for Spider. It was the gaudiest thing he had ever seen.

Spider was the last person Ricky wanted to ever see again, but for this moment, he had been counting the days, hours, and right up to the minute. Spider was now the most important means to an end to help his little girl, and Ricky was a changed man. He was confident, he was focused. He would never again fall for Spider's influence or alpha-aggression. He was too determined to get caught up in the web of Spider's charm.

"What's up, motherfucker!" Spider yelled as Ricky stepped down the bus's stairs into the blast of cold, dry desert air.

"Hey, Spidey, missed you, bro," Ricky reached out for a handshake. He couldn't muster a hug; it was hard enough to feign any enthusiasm whatsoever.

"Get in, my man, have I got some good shit to tell you." Ricky walked around to the passenger side while Spider put one hand on the closed door and the other on the T-top and leaped into his car *Dukes of Hazzard* style.

"So, $20,000 huh, I hope you ain't lying, man. I left my sick kid at home for this," Ricky reiterated in a serious tone.

"Yup!" Spider punched the gas and they peeled out of the bus station. "Let's discuss the plan over a drink."

As the Firebird sped down the strip, Ricky noticed it was especially quiet. He didn't know if it was the cold-ass weather and snow residue still melting along the sidewalks, or if it had just changed that much over the year he'd been gone. Maybe it was just that he was noticing things through sober eyes for the first time in years, or maybe he just didn't care enough about the town anymore to feel anything at all for it.

The car stopped in the parking lot of The Black Spade, a dingy bar seated in the shadows behind The Flamingo Casino. They had the cheapest drafts in town, and the two had spent many days in the dark belly of this beast when they couldn't find or afford any more entertaining means of getting buzzed.

"Would you look at that, our old spot is open." Spider pointed to the back-corner table next to an old, broken Kiss pinball machine. "It's fate." The two slithered into the booth, which had old black and white photos of Vegas from yesteryears on one wall and a more current poster of *The Good, the Bad and the Ugly.*

"All right, man, spill it. What the hell do you have cooked up?" Ricky was already growing impatient. This bar, which used to be a haven for him, was now a nightmare. It was a reminder of literally everything that was wrong with his past and everything he had worked so hard to remedy.

Just then, a look of sheer sincerity came over Spider's face. Ricky had only seen this look once before, when Spider was describing his incident at the Pink Shark Club years prior. Spider lived to be the life of the party and the fun-times guy, so he had but one serious bone in his body, and he typically used that to fuck with. *Damn, maybe this is actually legit,* Ricky thought.

"Okay fine. So hear me out before you say a word, dude," started Spider. "Last New Year's I was partying with this guy who was telling me he hadn't spent that much money since Christmas Eve. I was like, what, on your woman? He was like, fuck no, haha, at the titty bar! He told me it's the busiest night of the year, and he'd never seen so many strippers and lonely, depressed men. So, it got me thinking how much money the clubs made that night. I started casing clubs on nights before holidays, and they were all the same. Easter, Fourth of July, shit, even Valentine's Day, you name it, busy as hell. Thing is, titty bars only close on the holidays."

Ricky sighed and sank back into the booth, folding his arms. *This is a total waste of time.* A titty bar, or any pair of tits for that matter, were the furthest thing from his mind.

Spider leaned in close, surveyed the other patrons, and lowered his voice.

"So, all that money from the busiest times, the nights before the holidays, just sits in the club, unguarded the whole next day. Nobody would even know it's missing until the next business day. Banks are closed, the club is closed, owners are out with their families. So, I'm gonna take it, all of it! It's the easiest foolproof gig ever,"

Ricky laughed.

"And just how are you planning on doing that, dude? They probably have alarms and safes and all that, and you are a smash and grab guy; you don't know shit about that stuff."

"That's why we have Cinnamon."

"Haha, cinnamon, what the hell is that gonna do? You gonna magically sprinkle it on the cameras?" Ricky laughed at his own sarcasm.

"No, you smart ass. Cinnamon is a stripper there.".

Suddenly Ricky's laughter turned to intrigue. He unfolded his arms and scooted to the edge of the torn leather seat, leaning in to hear every word.

"I've known her a long time, and she is trustworthy. She's bitter and hates her job and the owner. We have been planning it for a month now. Everything is set, down to the last detail . . ." Spider looked Ricky right in the eyes. The most serious look Ricky had ever seen from him. ". . . and that's where you come in."

Ricky looked puzzled. He folded his arms and raised an eyebrow, "how is that where I come in?"

"Well, you see," Spider leaned in even closer, about eight inches away, eye to eye. "Cinnamon is smart, and knows waaaaay too much. So, I'll need you to take care of her."

"Take care of her? Like take care of her take care of her?" Ricky turned pale. He couldn't believe his ears.

"Yes." Spider's face showed no empathy, and his entire demeanor turned to complete indifference.

Ricky leaned even closer to Spider.

"Like kill her?" He already knew the answer but was in too much disbelief to accept it.

"It's the only loose end. That's all you have to do, make her disappear, and the $20,000 is yours. Five minutes of work to help your sick kid have a long life, man," Spider knew how to tug on Ricky's heartstrings, and he knew Ricky would do anything for his daughter. But murder? Where would he draw the line?

"I just figured you would do whatever it takes to save your little girl, man. Maybe I was wrong."

"What! No way. Why? Why can't you . . . why me?" stuttered Ricky.

"Because it needs to be done while I'm inside the club, before there's any ammunition against me, in case she tries to outsmart or double-cross me and takes the money for herself," answered Spider. "She's just too much of a liability, and let's face it, she's a whore bitch. She could blackmail us or do anything she wanted if tempted or angry. Do you want to worry about her or look over your shoulder the rest of your life?"

"But I thought you trusted her?" Ricky pondered.

"I trust her to do her job for this. I don't trust any person beyond that, especially some bitch. C'mon, man, she's still a fucking stripper!"

"I don't know, man. I just don't know, that's heavy. I wasn't expecting that. I gotta think about this a while, man." Ricky still wasn't ready to accept it yet. Plus, he needed time to think of his out, his getaway.

"I get it, bro, I know it's a lot to take in. This has to happen tomorrow night, though, Christmas Eve. So, let me know tonight. I need you, man. I need you for this to work perfectly, and you're the only one I trust anymore, the only one in the world, bro," said Spider. "I know you love your daughter enough to do this one thing for her."

"I'll call you tonight, man, I gotta weigh this." Spider nodded then got up and walked out of the diner. Ricky stayed frozen in the old booth. He couldn't believe he could commit murder. He stared at the movie poster on the wall, focusing on the gun imagery. He couldn't let the only true love in his life crumble and decay away right before his eyes any longer.

Ricky already knew he had to do it. It was his daughter's life or Cinnamon's.

11

"Bogey's Pad"
Las Vegas Suburbs
★ 1988 ★

There was a knock at the door, and several big black men immediately arose from the couch where they were watching *The Price Is Right*. Bogey stepped off his treadmill, unhappy that he was interrupted during a good run. He snatched a towel off the shelf to his right and slung it around his neck. Then he grabbed a gold-plated 9 mm off the coffee table and stuck it in his red Adidas pants, which was normal routine.

To Bogey's relief, a friendly, familiar face was on the other side of the door when his crew opened it. It was Ricky, his trusted and loyal old lackey.

"Holy shit, my nigga!" Bogey yelled with surprise. "Get yo tall, skinny honky ass in here."

"What's up, cuz, good to see you," said Ricky, who immediately eyeballed the gun peeking out of Bogey's track pants. Bogey noticed Ricky stare at his weapon, and he tucked it deeper into his pants to help him ease up a little. It was not an unusual sight; there were always guns, drugs, or money surrounding anything with Bogey or his house.

Ricky walked through the doorway and immediately scanned the scene. A couple gargantuan men lowered back down on the couch that was in the same place; they were just different men than before. That damn treadmill was still to his left, but now there was a giant ivory piano to his right. It looked like it must have cost a million bucks, and there was a tiger blanket lying under its bench seat. Bogey's decor had drastically elevated in value, and he was doing very, very well for himself. The curved staircase ahead had a gold railing leading up to the balcony which Ricky had never made it up to in all the times he had been there. The cliché art on the walls was now gone, replaced by expensive, framed vintage boxing match posters and athletes' autographed jerseys. Being from Florida, Ricky immediately noticed the Dolphins' Marino jersey and several more football and baseball collectibles ascending the stairs.

"I honestly thought I'd never see you again, man," Bogey admitted as he set his gun back on the coffee table. "Sit, sit," he said, beckoning to the white leather sofas.

"And I never thought I'd be back here, haha," Ricky laughed. "But desperate times and all, I need a quick job, dude."

"Damn, son, cut right to the chase. It's cool, it's cool, I can tell you gots shit going on. What kind of score you looking for?" joked Bogey.

"Transportation—fast transportation," Ricky said without

hesitation. He knew from the start that Bogey would be the only one who could help him disappear or get back to Florida quickly and quietly if everything went south. It would cost him, but Ricky would worry about that later. Bogey was his expensive insurance policy.

"Right on, man, I hear ya. I got just the job for you then," Bogey replied.

"And I need a gun," added Ricky with sweat collecting on his receding hairline.

"A gun!? Oh shit, Ricky, what you got yourself into, man? You sure you want to play up to the pro league and go down that route?" Bogey was actually surprised. In all the time he knew Ricky, he had never asked for a gun, carried a gun, or even looked twice at a gun. Now he knew just how serious Ricky really was.

"It's not what I got myself into, it's what I need to get myself out of," Ricky leaned toward Bogey, "then you'll never see me again."

"It's cool, man. I don't want to know, I don't need to know; you've never done me wrong, so I got the perfect job for you." Bogey stood up. "Follow me," he said as he turned toward the garage. They walked down the long hallway together, which was aligned with framed gold records. First Run DMC, then Public Enemy, then another rap album after another. These records alone were worth more than everything Ricky owned in his life combined. At the end of the hall Bogey opened a door to reveal one of the most beautiful sights Ricky had ever laid eyes on, way more impressive than the walk of rap fame he had just taken to get there.

"Brand-new Candy Apple Red 1988 Ford Mustang 5.0, bro, wooooooooo!" announced Bogey.

Ricky's jaw dropped.

"Holy shit."

"And I want you to take it," Bogey demanded.

"Excuse me?" Ricky was stunned.

"You heard me, brother. I want you to take this car and make it disappear. I can't have it here no mo. The IRS is all over me, threatening me, and I just lost a major client who went and got themselves killed. I can't be having no mo red flags around, they be watching me, and it is literally a bright red flag in yo face. So, I want you to steal this car from me."

"You want me to what from what?" Ricky was still stunned, partially by the beauty of the car, but mostly from the words coming from Bogey's mouth.

"Straight up, man, if you steal it and I report it, say two days later, it can turn up wrecked in a Florida swamp somewhere for all I care. All I want is the insurance money and fools off my back, not attracting any unneeded attention if you know what I mean," Bogey nudged Ricky with an elbow to the arm.

"Ahhhh, now I see." Ricky understood.

"But for the gun, you need to make a simple delivery for me tomorrow," added Bogey. Now Ricky knew that there was nothing simple about Bogey's so-called simple deliveries. They usually entailed drugs, guns, or money, or all three, and you'd be locked up for a long time if you got caught. But what choice did he have? Better yet, this was his quick getaway car home to Ashley. This is exactly what he needed.

This turned the tides in his favor, and he was now ready to

make that phone call to Spider with his answer.

"You got it, boss." Ricky finalized the deal with a hand-shake.

"I knew I could count on you, my man," Bogey moved toward a giant circular saw farther into the garage and opened up the panel on it. "There's already a gun in the glove box, and here's your delivery." Bogey pulled a brick of coke out of the saw and set it in a small mustard-yellow suitcase. "Take this to the parking lot behind Harrah's tomorrow night at 10:00 and look for a blue van. Bring me back their package and we are all good in the hood, my brotha."

"Then we're straight?" Ricky asked.

"Then we straight!"

12

"Bogey's Pad"
Las Vegas Suburbs
★ 1988 ★

Rolling down the strip at sunrise was something Ricky had never done before. It was absolutely breathtaking. He eye-balled the old, run-down Lucky Horseshoe Casino across the road for a cheap hotel option, he needed to recharge himself. Suddenly, he whipped into an abandoned parking lot to his right. He spotted a pay phone. He had to get this call back to Spider over with, so he could get a little sleep then start planning the most terrifying day of his life.

When he stepped out of the car, he couldn't believe what lay to his immediate right. He hadn't seen it from inside the car because it was covered with overgrown palm trees and unkempt landscaping. But now it was like a painful reminding slap in the face. Was it a sign? Was it fate telling him this was all a mistake? Or, was it a symbol that old things die and bright new things may one day blossom from the rubble of bad memories, like a giant new casino that would one day lay on this plot of land.

It was the Pink Shark Club, or what was left of it. You could just barely make out the word "Shark" on the pink sign, the other half of which was now lying on the ground below. The boarded-up doors and windows had so much graffiti that you couldn't see bare wood anymore. Weeds grew waist-high out of cracks in the pavement. It looked like this place had lain desolate and rotting since the day of Spider's rampage, and that may have been the case. It was now overlooked but would never be forgotten. Ricky turned toward the pay phone, hoping it still worked.

"I'm in," said Ricky, phone in hand.

"I knew you wouldn't let me down, Ricky," said Spider. "Meet me at the IHOP across from the Huge Venus at midnight. I'll go over everything then. Don't be late."

"I'll be there, dude." This was actually a perfect scenario for Ricky. Didn't sound like Spider had time to hang out before then, and Ricky had lots to do before midnight, which was now less than a day away.

Ricky got back in the car and headed across the street to check into a room for a few hours. He needed to clear his head and refresh. He had to carefully plan the next eighteen hours. First, he needed a little sleep, so he would be sharp and focused. Even though his nerves probably wouldn't allow it, he had to try and calm down. Then, he had to call his daughter. He needed to hear her voice, not only for motivation and direction, but just in case everything went south, and it was the last time they talked. After that, he had to plan the whole

Cinnamon thing—how and where it would take place and how and where to dispose of her. That meant he needed to drive around and find a suitable hiding or burying place. That had to be carefully coordinated with Bogey's package delivery meeting and drop off, all in time to get to the IHOP by midnight. Somehow, he needed to figure out an escape plan for after all was said and done.

This was already turning out to be the craziest day of his life, and it hadn't even begun yet. He pondered how his life had turned from easy and numb just a few days ago to what he got himself into now. He'd went from chopping down mangroves for some side cash to pay his rent to planning a heist, drug run, and murder.

13

"Christmas Deceive"

December 24
★ 10:10 AM ★

Ricky woke up in a puddle of his own sweat, even though it was cold as hell outside. It had to be from violent nightmares or premonitions he'd been having about the day before him. The hotel room reeked of mildew and cotton balls, and the Irish-green shag carpet was probably home to a million insects.

He reached toward the phone on the nightstand. It was Christmas Eve after all, and not being around Ashley for this particular day was already hurting his heart. He had missed a couple Christmases before, when he was completely fucked up on drugs, but it didn't hit him as hard then because what he'd cared about most during that time frame was his next high. Now that he was clean, it was tormenting his soul. He was also not oblivious to the fact that the very thing he was going to do to try and save her could be the same thing that put him away for life and separated them forever. The only consolation he felt was that his immoral actions may indeed save her innocent life, and that was all the righteousness he needed. A million thoughts flooded his head as he pressed each number on the phone.

"Hello," a squeaky little voice answered.

"Ashley, it's Daddy."

"Daddy! Where are you?"

"I had to leave for work, honey."

"Well, are you gonna be here to open a present with me to-night?" Ashley innocently asked. Ricky had promised Ashley for months that they would be able to open one present together Christmas Eve. A tear rolled down his cheek, and it took all his strength to not start crying.

"No, baby, I'm so sorry. I'm working for a doctor here, so we can make you better real soon. The only deal was that they needed daddy to do it right away."

"Really? Will he make me all better after you work for him?"

"Yes, baby, I promise. I will only be a couple days more, and then we will have our own special Christmas, okay? Do you understand that, baby?" Ricky had to make sure that Ashley wasn't too sad before he hung up and understood that he was only trying to help her. He was hoping she would understand the bigger picture, even if only in a small way.

"That's okay, Daddy. I understand. I can't wait to see you. Can I sleep over at your house when you come home?" Ricky's heart swelled.

"Of course, baby, we can make a fort and sleep together inside it all night with all your princesses, and whatever new toys Santa brings you; sound like a deal?" It sounded like a dream to Ricky. Unfortunately, he knew it was an unlikely dream at this point.

"Yay!" Ashley replied excitedly.

"Daddy's got to go work for the doctor for you now, okay? I love you so much," Ricky barely got out without breaking down.

"Love you too, Daddy. Bye Bye."

As soon as he hung up, he burst into a wave of tears. He'd hung up before Ashley could hear his sadness. He couldn't take another second of her innocent and perfect little voice.

The sadness was his drug now, though. That little girl was his motivation, his energy, and his sanity. Ricky jumped up and into the shower. He felt revived and ready. He finally felt a sense of confidence and hope.

14

"Big Fat Purple Thing"
December 24
★ 1:02-3:35 PM ★

The day was now actually warm enough to put the top down in Bogey's Mustang. This was a December heat wave like he'd never seen, and the fresh air blowing in his face kept Ricky sane. After all, he was literally driving around to find a perfect spot to dump a dead body. He just kept repeating one word in his head—Ashley, Ashley, Ashley—as he pulled into a Mc-Donalds drive-thru.

`There was no way the elimination of Cinnamon could be done in town. There were way too many people out and around the casinos at night, too much risk of being seen, even on Christmas Eve. He couldn't simply dispose of her in a dumpster or alley to be found later either; too much risk of fingerprints and such. He had to be smart about this. Smarter than he had ever been in his life. He didn't want anything tied to Cinnamon that would lead back to him or even worse, his daughter one day discovering what he'd done.

Ricky got his burger at the drive-thru window, and right as he'd started pulling out, two kids dashed in front of the car. Ricky braked.

"Hey! Look before you cross!"

The kids ignored him and ran to the Grimace slide in the play area. Then he saw it.

It wasn't the big, fat, purple cartoon character slide that he actually took notice to, but what was behind it. Peeking out just between the Hamburglar-go-round and that ugly purple whatever-it-was were the rolling desert hills just outside of town. Like a beacon of light, Ricky saw the exact spot he needed to go. He tore open his McDLT, threw the Styrofoam container in the back seat, smashed a huge bite, and rocketed out of there.

His mind was now running faster than his Mustang. First stop was to the hardware store. He needed a shovel for the hole and lime to mask the smell, so the coyotes wouldn't dig the body up. He saw those details in a movie once and they seemed logical. He needed a tarp or plastic sheeting to line the trunk with, so there would be no blood trail. If he had any money left, he would've also liked to buy a couple potted plants and a bag of fertilizer, so that it would look like he was planning a nice day of gardening rather than a night of murderous villainy. But he didn't have the funds for any of that, so just the killing supplies it would be.

15

"Caesar's Palace"

Check-in Desk
★ 7:49 PM ★

"How can I help you, sir?"

The receptionist stood behind the fancy marble countertop.

"I'd like a room for tonight, ma'am," replied the gentleman, pulling his hat down a little lower. He kept his head angled ever-so-slightly down so the shadow cast from his hat hid his eyes just enough.

"What's the name, sir?" It wasn't an odd occurrence that someone in this town, spending this kind of money, didn't want to be seen or recognized. "And do you have a floor or view preference?"

"No, ma'am, just a view of you." The stranger nodded and tipped his hat with a wink. "The name is Ricky. Ricky North."

The receptionist cracked a smile and blushed a little but didn't have the confidence to reply. "Can I offer you a free beverage coupon for the bar, Mr. North? We appreciate you here at Caesar's Palace."

"Thanks, darlin', and believe me, I appreciate you." Mr. North pulled out several hundred-dollar bills. "I'd like to just pay cash for everything up front, you know, in case I have too wild of a night and forget."

The receptionist was easily flustered, and handed him his change without even bothering to check an ID. "Here's your key, Mr. North. Room 1251. Enjoy your stay."

"Thank you kindly," the mystery man replied. As he walked away, all the receptionist noticed were his flamboyant snakeskin boots clicking and clacking on the Italian marble floor.

16

"The Job Before the Job"
Parking Lot Behind Harrah's
★ 9:52 PM ★

All Ricky could think about was the small mustard-yellow suitcase in the trunk. He would just have to do the speed limit and hope for the best. Ricky took every corner with complete caution, coming to complete stops at all signs.

It wasn't hot enough out to sweat, but Ricky certainly was—in buckets. What the fuck was wrong with him? He'd done all kinds of shit like this for Bogey before. But it had no meaning or consequences he gave a shit about back then; that was the difference, and his heart knew it. His heart was almost beating right out of his chest. Ricky couldn't remember a single time in his life that he was this nervous. He had no idea what he was driving into.

He checked his watch as he turned into the designated meeting point behind Harrah's Casino. Perfect, it was 9:52. He had a few minutes to chill and let his balls drop before the exchange. But then he noticed a navy van in the darkened corner spot. He could barely move. He felt the anxiety creeping in. He needed a jolt, something to get his ass out of that seat. He reached in his front pocket and pulled out a Polaroid picture of Ashley that they had taken on the pier that day they got ice cream. That did it . . . like an adrenaline shot to the heart. His whole demeanor changed. He had this. Fuck it!

He stopped about fifteen feet in front of the van. He slowly got out, exposing his empty hands, then tugging up his shirt a little to confirm that he had nothing concealed in the waistband of his pants. He knew the drill.

Two big guys immediately got out of the van. They looked like a WWF tag-team champion duo that got cut for being too scary for prime-time TV.

"Who are you?" demanded the more-heavily tattooed one. Just the sound of his deep voice would make any average man quiver at the knees like a little bitch.

"I'm Ricky."

"Am I supposed to know or care who the fuck Ricky is? Where's Bogey?" The giant clenched his fists.

"Hahaha," Ricky chuckled. "Bogey doesn't make his own deliveries. He's too important to do that," Ricky said in a sarcastic tone to ease tension. "He sent me. I got your package in my trunk."

"Go get it . . . slowly . . . and bring it here," said the other giant as his partner pulled his leather jacket aside to expose a gun, making sure Ricky could see it.

Ricky backstepped slowly but with confidence. He raised his hands in the air to show his intent to follow orders. He had been in some tricky situations before because of Bogey, but never anything like this. Oddly enough, though, a temporary calm came over him. He still had too much to do for this to all go south now.

"No problem, guys." He slowly raised the trunk lid. *Oh fuck.* He peered over the trunk to double-check the guys' location. The trunk looked like it had been prepped to murder these guys and run off with everything. The interior was lined with plastic and a shovel and a bag of lime. If they saw any of this, he was surely dead. He quickly grabbed the suitcase and raised it in sight with one hand, slowly pulling the trunk closed with the other. Again, he raised his free hand to show he was bearing no weapon or ill intent, and he placed the suitcase on the ground by his feet.

"Okay, here it is, where's Bogey's return?" Ricky now felt all the confidence in the world; he had to with these guys or they would eat him alive. He nudged the case toward the giants with a slight kick. *Moment of truth,* Ricky thought. They were either gonna accept it and do the deal, or take it and leave him there dead. There was nothing he could do to stop that now.

The giant closest to Ricky stopped the sliding suitcase with his foot and slowly leaned over to find the latches. He took a knee and peered inside it. A smile came over his face until he realized it and caught himself, quickly transforming back to his tough-guy scowl. He turned toward the van and nodded at the dark window. Ricky couldn't see whom he was nodding at, nor did he care. He just wanted to get the fuck out of there.

Just then the van door rolled open just enough for a skinny arm with a loose gold watch dangling from it to slide out. The arm held out a tan briefcase for the other mountainous brute to come grab. The big lackey turned and walked it over to Ricky.

"Please tell Mr. Bogey it's a pleasure doing business with him, and we look forward to more opportunities." It was like he had been rehearsing that line all day in his puny brain but hadn't been allowed to say it until everything went as planned.

An enormous weight lifted from Ricky's shoulders. He practically floated back to his car, threw the briefcase in the back seat, and got the fuck outta there.

17

"Cinnamon's Last Stand"

Las Vegas
★ 10:21 PM ★

Sitting at the stoplight in her beat-up gold Datsun, Cinnamon adjusted the rearview mirror to reapply her fire-engine red lipstick. She was running late. It was always the same scenario—comfy at home watching classic love-story movies while cooking dinner. She would get lost in the fairy-tale worlds of what she wished her life could one day be. It was virtually impossible to pull herself away from that peace to face the pieces of shit that were waiting for her at the club. Feeling warm and innocent at home always had to give way to feeling old, sweaty perverted hands on her thighs. She dreaded it every night. Cinnamon loathed this existence. But tonight, she was behind pace for a different reason. Deciding on the last-minute clothes and sentimental items that she couldn't live without made her lose track of time.

Tonight was different from any typical night. Tonight

would be either her justice or judgment. After this long night she would be done with the stripper life forever, whether it ended with enough cash to get out of this life or the darkness of Spider's betrayal taking her life. Whatever happened, she promised herself that this would be the last time she ever pulled into the dank parking lot of the Huge Venus.

She'd packed up just the essentials before leaving her apartment. Just a few old Schlitz Beer boxes of mementos and dishes and a big duffel bag of clothes sat in the corner awaiting her return. She was gonna do this one last night, and God willing, come home, pack up her car, and hit the road to any-fucking-where but here. One last time at the shitty night club, followed by one more time at her shitty apartment above the record store, then off to a new life, wherever that took her.

She passed the IHOP and turned into the Huge Venus. The phallic neon lights lit up half the street, even part of the damn pancake house across from it. She pulled into the employee parking in back and turned off the engine.

"Get out of the car, Cinnamon," she said to herself. "You can do this. One night, just one more night." Squeezing the turning wheel, her hands started turning as red as her bright fingernails. She didn't dare look in her rearview because she knew that one look at the fright she couldn't hide on her face and she would break down. *Smile and get out of the fucking car right now!* She looked down and adjusted her tits to plump them up in her bra and opened the door . . .

"Driving Back to Bogey's House"
Las Vegas Suburbs
★ 10:21 PM ★

Ricky pulled to the curbside a block away from his target. Now was the time to be extra careful. Since this car was going to be reported stolen in the morning, he didn't want anyone seeing him in it, especially pulling into Bogey's driveway. Ricky's mind was sharp, and he was at the top of his game. Being guided by love for once in his life made all the difference on spontaneous choices.

He glided like a ghost toward Bogey's place, light-footed and nearly invisible, even being careful to not leave as much as a footprint in the lush green lawn by the entry. He was gonna drop this briefcase in Bogey's hands and get the fuck out of there forever.

Suddenly, he stopped in his tracks. The front door was ajar. The light that was peering out of the cracked opening looked like the most dangerous beacon of get-the-fuck-away he'd ever seen in his life. Every fiber of his mind told him to cut his losses and get the hell out of there. But he couldn't listen to his mind right now; he had to follow his heart and do whatever it took for Ashley. He took a big breath.

He carefully nudged the door open with his fingertips. He looked behind himself first to double-check his surroundings, then slowly peered inside. Just as he was wondering if he should call out Bogey's name, he saw that he didn't need to . . . ever again.

Ricky first noticed the contrast of the dark red on the glistening marble floor. Then his eyes followed the mahogany trail to Bogey's body. He was slumped over his treadmill, arms and head arched over the controls and legs dragging on the platform. His white Adidas tracksuit was sopping with red stain, and a pool of blood had collected on the tread below. The blood was weighing down the fabric, exposing several stab wounds. Somebody wanted to leave a gruesome message about Bogey. But how did anyone do this; he was so well protected! Where were his henchmen? Maybe they were the ones who did it! Whoever it was meant for could surely be here soon, if not already. Or the cops!

"Oh fuck me," Ricky said. "Fuck this." Before he could even think about moving, his natural reflexes kicked in and his legs started running toward the door, hands still holding tightly to the briefcase. He made it to the driveway and stopped in his tracks, almost falling backward. *I touched the door*, his criminal mind reminded him. He hustled back and pulled up his shirt to wipe off the area where he pushed the door open. Then he turned back toward the driveway and sprinted down the street to his car.

Ricky threw the briefcase in his trunk and jumped in the car. He sat still and frozen with anxiety. *Turn the key, Ricky, turn the key,* he kept telling himself. His eyes surveyed his dark surroundings. He still couldn't move. Side to side, in the rear-view, and down the street in front of him he kept looking. *No dark figures in parked cars . . . check. Nobody sneaking around any yards . . . check. Nobody peering through any windows . . . check.* It was dead silent. With his mental checklist done, his wrist finally started twisting the key. He was cautious to start the engine as slowly as possible without giving the powerful engine too much gas. He didn't want to wake up any neighbors or create any attention his way. With the car at a gentle hum, he put it in gear and eased away, keeping the headlights off until he got to a main intersection. Ricky started breathing again.

As he noticed some different kind of bright lights coming toward him he turned the corner toward the bright lights of the Strip and flipped on his headlights. Just as he'd started settling down, his heart was hit with a shot of nerves and began pounding through his chest. Three red and blue flashing lights were flying right toward him. *Holy fuck, I'm done, what do I do.* A million emotions raced through his head instantaneously, and a hundred scenarios of what to do or not do. He had about three seconds to either pull aside or take a corner to outrun them. *But how could they know it was me, did somebody report this car, did somebody actually see me leaving? I was so careful. The thoughts continued to race. But wait, I didn't do anything wrong! Wait, fuck, I just did a drug deal for him, maybe those guys ratted us out?*

At the last possible second, Ricky pulled the Mustang to the side of the street and put his hands on the top of the wheel. *I am just gonna face the consequences and tell the truth. They don't know what I did, I did nothing wrong. I went to visit a friend and found him dead, got scared, and ran off, that's all.* The cop cars were almost upon him. Any second now. *God damnit,* his thoughts argued, *I am in a stolen car with a bag from a drug deal in back. I have no time to ditch either. Oh my God, I am totally . . .*

Just then the three police cars raced by him. They didn't even look in his direction. Ricky's heart began beating again. Was luck actually on his side? Ricky looked in his rearview mirror and saw the squad car brake. *Fuck, maybe not.* But then the rear red lights started blinking. The black and whites all took sharp turns onto Bogey's street. *They were going to the scene of the crime, holy shit.* Ricky didn't know how they'd found out about it and frankly didn't even care at this point. His luck had resumed. Half of this terrible night was over, but the worst part still lay before him.

"IHOP"

Christmas
★ 12:04 AM ★

Spider sat in the corner booth with a half-eaten Rooty Tooty Fresh and Fruity meal in front of him. The pancake house was typically packed at this hour with drunks, homeless, and gamblers fueling up to blow a load. But tonight, it was dismal. Maybe four patrons shared the restaurant with Spider. It was quiet, almost peaceful.

Spider quickly looked up from his meal each time the front door chimed open. He was high as hell and noticeably twitchy. His watch read 12:02, then 12:03, 12:04. *Where the fuck was . . .*

Just then the door opened to reveal Ricky. He looked flustered. Ricky located Spider and walked toward him at a quick pace. He slid into the booth and faced Spider, anticipating a verbal lashing.

"You're late, dude."

"Sorry, man, got stuck behind an accident. I'm here, brother, all good now," Ricky explained. "Almost forgot how bad the traffic was in this town, even at midnight."

"I was starting to wonder if you pussed out; you're never late. You ready for this then? Pay close attention. I have it all planned out to the T." Spider leaned in and slowed down. "I've been working on this for months. Everything is all set." He lowered his voice.

"Give it to me. I'm ready, boss."

"All right. So don't look now, but the titty bar across the street was my usual hangout for a long time. I know every inch of it, as does Cinnamon. Anyway, after many, many lap dances with this Cinnamon, I got this brilliant idea, and she's the only person that can help us."

"I still can't believe you're trusting a stripper," Ricky said.

"Cinnamon hates it there, hates the owner, hates the job, all of it. She got robbed. She's weak and miserable. She's the perfect mark," Spider resumed.

"Yeah you told me all that already," added Ricky.

"Exactly! She knows where they stash the cash. She's seen it. Cinnamon said she overheard the owner bragging to a coworker that last Christmas Eve he made almost $40,000! The owner isn't even here this week, on vacation in Rio or some shit, so it will be even longer than normal! We gotta smoke the moment, man, smoke this moment."

"Makes sense. I get it. But how you gonna pull it off?" wondered Ricky. "I'm sure they have lots of cameras, or alarms. And look at that place; there's not a window, it's like a damn sex fortress."

"Way ahead of you, dude. Cinnamon is gonna disable the cameras. There's no alarm. It's broken, also thanks to our lovely lady. I am gonna go to the bathroom before closing and hide up in the ceiling. I already looked weeks ago, and there's enough room above the acoustic ceiling tiles. When they lock up and leave, I just climb down, walk in the office, and grab the cash, and walk out the backdoor. My car is hidden, parked a half block away." Spider glanced around to double-check that none of the staff were listening. "So, you take care of Cinnamon after she leaves the club, and I'll do all this here. We will meet at Caesar's Palace room 1251, when it's all said and done. I'll give you your cut, and you can go help your daughter, and we both vanish from this town forever."

Spider's plan actually sounded virtually foolproof, even for his dumb ass.

"Well, it sounds like you got it all figured out, dude," Ricky continued. "I'll be there, man, don't you worry. Room 1251. See you then." Ricky reached over and grabbed a strawberry off of Spider's plate and popped it in his mouth as he stood up. "Room 1251, good luck, bro."

"This is gonna change your life, dude! See you there," Spider reassured Ricky one last time, even though Ricky didn't need it or care at this point.

20

"The Huge Venus"

Inside

★ 2:18 AM ★

Spider stood up from his seat in front of the main stage. He slammed back one last shot of Jack and pounded the glass upside down beside the four other empty ones in front of the brass bar circling the stage.

He turned and walked down the rear hall, right behind a tall blonde. His eyes were fixated on the nicest ass he'd ever seen: milky white skin that formed two flawless round cheeks sticking out from underneath some purple lace. So tight and smooth, each cheek bounced perfectly with every step. He wished he could stay in this slow-motion moment forever. For a second, his fixation made him forget he had a job to do. As she turned left to the dressing room he returned to reality and turned right, into the men's room.

After sitting in the last stall for a few, Spider allowed the liquor to calm his raging boner. That blonde's ass was permanently entered into his spank bank vault forever.

"Last call. Last call for alcohol." Spider overheard from the speakers outside the bathroom.

"Coming to the main stage for the last time tonight, the fiery hotness of Sinful Cinnnnamonnnn! Guys, let your dollars fly and keep your zippers high," the sleazy DJ announced in a stereotypical snake-like tone.

That was Spider's cue. The coast was clear, nobody else was in the bathroom, and the club was clearing out soon. Spider stood up on the toilet seat and popped up the ceiling tile above him. He slid it to the side and jumped up to grab the sprinkler pipe above it. He pulled himself up like an Olympian; after all, he was chasing gold. He kicked each foot over to a truss to balance himself, then slid the tile back into place. Now he waited.

Spider was left alone with his intoxicated thoughts. He knew he was a different breed than Ricky, or most people for that matter. He didn't know of anxiety at all. He didn't have worry or fear, or really concern himself with consequences from his actions, or think his actions even had consequences. The incident at the Pink Shark permanently singed any emotional pressure to follow society's unwritten moral guidelines. He almost felt invincible after making it through the hell and back he so publicly experienced years ago. In short, he was numb.

21

"The Huge Venus"
Outside
★ 2:29 AM ★

"She's got the looks that kill, that kill, she's got the looks that kill , she's got the look. . ."

Ricky loved this song. He needed this song right now to take his mind off what he was about to do. He tapped his fingers on the steering wheel to the beat of Tommy Lee's bass drum.

He circled the block once to check his surroundings and also find a good spot to park out of plain sight. Even though he wasn't really doing anything illegal at this site, he didn't want to be seen around this club at all. This was time to have absolute caution. He stayed on the street behind the club; *this was perfect*, he thought. He was hidden behind a pale-yellow truck and could still see the backdoor between the bushes and through the chain-link fence. Now it was time to wait. By Spider's description, Cinnamon wouldn't be hard to miss.

Just a little longer, Ricky tried to reassure himself, just a few more hours and this will all be over.

Back Inside
★ 2:39 AM ★

The bathroom door swung open, and a huge tattooed guy in a sleeveless leather jacket entered. He had spiked graying hair and looked like he ate children for protein snacks before hitting the gym. Spider could see his every move through a crack in the ceiling tile. This dude would crush him with no effort whatsoever if he found him. Spider's breathing was slow and calm, he didn't miss a beat. The only thing moving was the equilibrium inside his head, but that was from the Jack Daniel's, not nerves.

The bouncer gently kicked open each stall door, probably to check for drunken stragglers. He quickly exited after his rounds, and Spider heard an "all clear" come from the hallway.

Back Outside
★ 2:46 AM ★

The steel backdoor opened and several girls stumbled out

at once. Strippers were definitely hotter on the stage and under the complimenting lights. They were swaying back and forth and hanging on each other's shoulders for support. Ricky couldn't hear if it was laughter or bitching, but they were definitely animated about something. Most of them seemed as drunk now as their customers were in the club.

All except one. One was breaking away from the cackling pack on an obvious mission. As hugs and drunken goodbyes were being exchanged by trashy sluts behind her, she didn't even look back as one of the girls called out, "Bye, Cinny honey;" she just beelined to her car.

She was maybe one hundred pounds; what Ricky would call a spinner. There was not an ounce of fat on her tiny frame, yet she still had great curves in all the right places. But the hair. The hair is what did it for him. It was like a sunset got trapped under a halo. Her hair was like liquid fire dancing off her shoulders, hiding a porcelain angel's face.

Damn, Ricky thought, *this is the hottest chick I've ever seen.* This woman was nothing like your typical trashy stripper; no wonder Spider marked her. In a different time or place, this chick would be a Hollywood starlet, dancing on the silver screen, not on a brass pole.

She got in her old Datsun, and Ricky started up his Mustang. He was careful to wait a few seconds until he pulled out.

Back Inside
★ 3:13 AM ★

He waited until there was total silence to be sure that the club was empty. "Fuckin finally," Spider whispered under his breath. He was a sweaty mess. His arms felt like soft noodles from holding him up for almost an hour.

He slid the tile over and grabbed the sprinkler pipe to swing down, but his hands were way too sweaty. They lost grip instantly and he fell hard to the ground, catching the toilet-paper holder in the ribs on the way down. A few ceiling tiles came down with him and shattered to pieces upon impact with the floor. There was a chalky mess everywhere. He stood up and grabbed his hurt side. His hand had blood on it when he pulled it away. It dripped between his fingers and clotted instantly when it hit the dusty ceiling tile debris on the ground. He swung open the stall and stumbled over to the sink. He grabbed some hand towels, stuffed them under his shirt, and exited the bathroom without a care in the world. There was way too much adrenaline and alcohol pumping through his body to slow him down now.

He got to the office and opened the door. Cases of Jack Daniel's and Smirnoff inhibited the door from opening all the way. It was a den of disgust. There were haphazardly placed stacks of porno mags in every corner, and posters of pussy on the walls. Dozens of records formed a leaning tower of vinyl on the file cabinets, and a mountain of Lucky Strike cartons balanced on top of the security TVs, which were off thanks to Cinnamon's premeditated sabotage. But none of this was what Spider was looking for. He was searching for just one thing. One big, beautiful, beastly thing to change his life forever. His blood was now sifting through his fingers and leaving a small trail on the floor, but he was too wired to take notice.

He surveyed all four walls and found what he was looking for hanging behind him, above the door like a monstrous God. It was a giant Texas steer—a bull killed in its masculine prime and posted up as a trophy for life. Spider grabbed the desk chair and slid it underneath the beast. He grabbed it by the horns and yanked hard. It hinged open from the wall. There was nothing behind it. No safe, no hole in the wall.

"That fucking cunt, Cinnamon! She said it was here!" he cursed. "I'll kill her myself! Fucking bitch!" He slammed the bull head back against the wall and jumped off the chair. The bull ricocheted off of the wall and careened back open. All of a sudden, a Pittsburgh Steelers duffel bag fell out of the bull and touched down to Spider's feet.

"What the fuck," he said, bewildered. He knelt down and unzipped the bag to discover a treasure of fifties. He sifted his hand through the thicket of bills, and it was the greatest sensation his fingers had ever felt. Spider investigated the steer further and discovered a hole carved in the backside of its head that revealed a massive hiding place. It wasn't just a hole in the animal, but the entire head was carved out. He then noticed an obstruction toward the front of the hollowed-out core, right behind its nose. He reached in to withdraw a purple felt Crown Royal bag. When he pulled open the golden tassels his eyes widened. He emptied a pile of diamond rings and necklaces into his palm of dried blood. It was literally a pirate's treasure trove of jewelry: gold necklaces, wedding rings, and watches, lots of expensive watches.

Spider quickly dumped the contents back into the purple

liquor bag and threw it into the Steelers duffel. He slung the bag over his shoulder and stepped over to the filing cabinet to grab the Van Halen 1984 record sitting on top of the stack that he'd noticed earlier. He turned and ran out the backdoor, leaving only a trail of his own blood.

22

"A New Plan"

Cinnamon's Apartment
★ 3:13 AM ★

Cinnamon picked up her first box to take out to her car. Her freedom was so close at hand, but she felt no less at ease. Her mind just kept coming up with scenarios of what could go wrong with Spider at the club. The box was half her size, completely covering her line of sight. She turned sideways to open the door with her fingertips and caught it with her toes. Suddenly, something shoved the box from outside in, and a tall, skinny man came bursting through the door, slamming and locking it behind him.

Cinnamon fell to the floor, and the box fell on top of her, splashing out a stack of old photo albums and books that slid across the floor. She raised her hands up in defense and started to cry frantically, gasping to catch breaths. This was it. She knew it. She should have gone with her gut and not trusted that Spider. She just knew he would double-cross her, but the allure of escaping this lifestyle had been too strong.

"Please don't hurt me. Please, I'll do whatever you want, take whatever you want," Cinnamon begged.

Ricky knelt down right beside her and pulled out his gun. He put it to her head. He was no less nervous than Cinnamon but couldn't show it. The barrel was pressing against her beautiful hair. That sexy, long, fiery hair that mesmerized him when he first saw her exit the club.

Ricky fought the urge to look at her face. He grunted and strained to pull the trigger, but he just couldn't. She was too beautiful. She was unique, and she belonged in this world. He looked into her eyes, brown just like his daughter's. He looked away a split second to gather courage, took a deep breath, then refocused. He immediately saw her fear. And then it hit him.

She was also somebody's daughter.

Somebody else was out there who loved her, who would do anything for her. Where they were, who knows, but Ricky felt certain they would show up if they knew she was in trouble. What would his own daughter think if he killed someone else's daughter for her?

He lowered the gun and put his finger against her lips. Then he slowly helped her up.

She was a quivering ball of fear and could barely stand. Ricky helped her to the couch.

"Okay, just be quiet and listen and we will both walk out of here, okay?" he whispered.

"O-ooo-o-k-kay," Cinnamon barely got out. But there was something in his voice that was almost calming and sincere.

"Listen. Spider sent me here to kill you, to tie up any loose ends. I can't do that. I'm not a killer. I have a daughter of my own. That's the only reason I even agreed to do it, cause she's very sick and I was desperate for the money to make her better," Ricky tried to explain as briefly as possible. "I'm not gonna hurt you, okay?"

"Okay," Cinnamon said more calmly. There was something about this man. She couldn't put her finger on it, but he already seemed more trustworthy than Spider ever was.

"We can still make this work. What did Spider tell you to do afterward?" Ricky asked.

"He said to meet him at noon at Yak's outside of town, and he would pay me $5,000," Cinnamon claimed with tears. "I should have known, I'm so stupid," she was shaking her head while trying to hold back more tears.

"No, you're not stupid, it's okay. Spider has a cunning way to get people to do things. TRUST ME, I KNOW!" Ricky paused to think and ran his hands through his thinning hair, clutching it at the ends.

"I got a plan! I'll get you your money," Ricky continued, "go get a room at The Flamingo; it's busy and nothing about you will stand out or be noticed. I will finish up with Spider and come get you there. You can leave town with me, and I'll drop you off somewhere on my way. You disappear forever, and Spider will never know that I didn't complete my job. I know it's hard, but you gotta trust me." Ricky grabbed her shoulders and looked right into her eyes. "What other choice do we have? If you got to the cops, we are all dead. I think you know that now. Spider will kill us."

23

"Double-Down DoubleCross"

Caesar's Palace

★ 3:59 AM ★

Ricky quickly found a perfect parking spot at Caesar's, right by the exit. *Great start,* he thought, *maybe my luck will actually improve by morning.* He took one final look at his daughter's picture in his front pocket, bottling up the emotion to give him just enough juice to make it through this last part of the night. This was it, just one more thing to do. He couldn't believe he had already made it this far, and he was now so close. He took a second to pray that the night would finish in his daughter's favor. Ricky was not one to ask the higher power for anything; he knew that with a lifetime of disobedience he didn't deserve that right. But this time was different; it wasn't about him making money or making it out with his own life. It was about his daughter's life. This entire turn of events today could possibly have been the only time in his life that Ricky had had a single thought that wasn't selfish.

The grandeur of the lobby didn't faze Ricky a bit when he entered, he was totally sober and focused, and eager to get the fuck out of there. He went straight to the reception desk. He had a preconceived plan in mind. Ricky figured that he would get his own room just in case things went south and he had to hide out a minute. Better to be safe than sorry.

"I'd like a single for one night, please," Ricky asked the neatly dressed countergirl.

"Yes, sir, I'd be happy to help you with that. Can I have your name, please." Ricky said his name, and she started typing, but then stopped.

"Mr. North, it seems you already checked in earlier today. You are in room 1251."

Ricky was stunned. *Did that motherfucker Spider put the room under my name? Was he trying to set me up and betray me before the heist even happened? Think fast, Ricky, answer the lady . . .*

"Um sorry, I've had a little too much to drink, haha. I meant to ask if my friend has checked in yet. My old high school buddy, Richard Maximo, is supposed to meet me and I can't find him . . . again, probably cause I've drunk too much."

"Let me check . . . no, sir, no Richard Maximo. I'm sorry," replied the receptionist who wasn't the slightest bit disrupted by Ricky's actions.

"What about Spider Maximo, he likes everyone to call him 'Spider'?" Ricky came back.

"No, sir, sorry, nothing under a 'Spider' either."

"Okay, thanks, so sorry to bother you, ma'am. Could I just get another key then? I lost mine somewhere between playing craps and taking one, haha." Ricky wasn't subtle, but he was funny and charming, and it didn't usually take much effort for him to get what he needed from the ladies.

"No problem at all, sir, it happens all the time. Good luck," the woman said with the upmost politeness.

Ricky walked away with pretend inebriation in his step. *That motherfucker is either trying to set me up or lay blame on me if he gets caught. I gotta get my money and get the hell out of this city. I gotta find . . .* just as his thought escaped him, he heard a loud carrying laugh that he knew all too well. That obnoxious voice that loved to hear itself could only be Spider.

Sure enough, as his eyes followed the trail his ears picked up on, he saw Spider, acting like a fool at a blackjack table. Ricky could tell from across the casino floor that Spider was completely wasted. He was yelling and slamming money down on the table. The other players had already scooted their stools away from his obnoxious bubble. He was attracting the exact kind of attention they didn't need tonight. The smoking Asian man at the starting position of the table was rubbing his forehead above his glasses and shaking his head trying to stay quiet. And the fat Texan at the opposite end was pulling down on the brim of his hat, trying to hide from the embarrassment. The dealer was even looking around the pit, probably to gesture for security. Spider's mouth was running faster than the giant stack of chips he was burning through. *What a fucking idiot.*

I've gotta get him away from that table before he burns through all our cash, or even worse, gets us caught by bragging or running his mouth. Ricky started walking toward the commotion, but something in him changed his course at the last second. He tucked his face into his jacket and snuck right past Spider, behind a row of chromed-out Lucky 7s slot machines. He realized it would just be safer and easier to go straight to the room and see if there was any money left up there. Then he could snatch it and get the fuck away from Spider.

Ricky eagerly hopped into the elevator when it landed, but not before Spider looked up. They locked eyes just before the door shut. Spider feverishly gathered all his chips and shoved them into every pocket possible. As he left the table in a hurry, the dealer caught him with, "Sir, what about your standing bet?" "Fuck off," Spider snarled under his breath as he practically ran toward the elevator.

By this time security had caught on to Spider's disruptive behavior and had been already on their way to give him a warning at the table. They immediately changed direction when they saw him scramble toward the elevator and continued to follow him.

24

"A Web of Lies"
Room 1251, Caesar's Palace
★ 4:20 AM ★

Room 1251 was a complete mess. There were half-snorted lines on the nightstand and empty beer bottles thrown about. A pile of bloody clothes was at the foot of the bed. There was a coil of blood-soaked towels by the bathroom door and a spilled ice bucket on the TV stand.

Ricky was in awe. He felt chills down his spine, like he'd just entered a crime scene. Before he could even process anything further, the door slammed open behind him.

"Ricky, you made it!" Spider shouted. "About damn time."

"Yeah, I'm here, bro, that Cinnamon thing was a harder job than I thought. Guess I'm outta shape, haha,"

"Oh really. I thought you had all that planned out during the day," Spider accused Ricky as he nudged past him.

"Yeah, man, had to be sure, ya know."

"Really? I think you just might be lying, dude; your hands

or clothes aren't even sweaty or dirty," accused Spider, wiggling his finger side to side.

"Well, what are you lying about, Spider? What's with the bloody clothes? What's with putting this room under my name? What the fuck are you up to, man?" Ricky challenged him.

A devilish grin came across Spider's face followed by a sarcastic chuckle. "The heist was a bust, man. I couldn't find the money, all I got was chump change. Here's your cut," Spider reached in his pocket and threw a few hundred-dollar chips at Ricky's feet. "Be glad you get that much." Spider went over to a desk and leaned against it. Ricky then noticed Spider slowly sliding a duffel farther underneath it with his foot.

"Really, what's in the bag behind your feet then?" Ricky hadn't come this far to take any shit. He had been through too much today to leave empty-handed.

"Listen, I know you pussied out on Cinnamon, and now I gotta clean up your mess, so you don't get another penny, dude." Spider opened his denim jacket to reveal a gun tucked into his pants. "Just leave now and go home and there won't be any problems, old friend. You even think about ratting me out, and I'll come find your daughter in Florida and a surgery will be the least of your worries."

Ricky was stunned. He wanted to scream so many things at the top of his lungs, but a calm intelligence came over him when he thought of his daughter. He took a deep breath. Now the vision of not being at her bedside was worse than any other scenario he could picture. At this point he just had to get out of this mess and away from this lunatic forever. Then an idea came to him.

"Fine, fine, old friend, you win," Ricky conceded. "You'll never hear from me again, just leave my daughter out of this. Thanks for nothing, man, have a good life. Karma is a cruel bitch you'll have to face one day, Spider," Ricky slowly bent over and grabbed the chips off the floor.

"Smart move, Ricky. You're lucky I don't end you here and now. The only reason I'm not is because of all the good times we've had together. I don't ever want to hear your name . . ."

Before Spider could finish his arrogant sentence, Ricky threw the chips as hard as he could at Spider's face. When Spider raised his hands to block them, Ricky dove for him like Lawrence Taylor sacking a vulnerable quarterback. Ricky went for the gun first and managed to get it out of Spider's pants. Ricky spun the gun around in his hand and slammed the butt of it against Spider's forehead, opening his skin up like a can of tomato sauce. Spider was stunned and slumped over on the floor.

"You'll never be anything more than alone, Spider.

Without wasting a single second Ricky hopped up and grabbed the duffel from under the desk. He turned to exit the room and walked as fast as he could down the hall. Waiting for the elevator was the longest ten seconds of his life. As the steel door began to slide closed, the elevator next to him simultaneously opened, and two big security guards stepped out. Just before Ricky's elevator sealed shut, he heard a scream from down the hall . . .

"Ricky! Ricky, I'm gonna kill you!"

The two security guards took off running toward the

sound. When they rounded the corner, they collided with a bloody mess of a man coming from the other direction. It was Spider, profusely bleeding from the forehead. The first security guard tried wrapping up Spider, but he weaseled out of it and kicked in the guard's knee, sending him straight to the floor. Spider then smashed the other guard up against the wall and managed to snatch his gun. Without hesitation or a single thought of remorse Spider put the gun to the guard's belly and pulled the trigger. He then turned to the guard getting up from the floor and placed the gun against his temple, this time triggering two shots.

It was the Pink Shark Club all over again, but this time without any alibis or claims of temporary insanity. This was a new symphony of greed and survival, and Spider was the conductor of chaos.

Casino Floor
Caesar's Palace
★ 4:39 AM ★

The elevator doors slid apart to reveal four more security guards and cops waiting on the other side. Ricky's body told him to freeze, but his mind made his feet take a few steps forward and exit. He stepped out as calmly as he possibly could, trying to muster an innocent, shocked look.

"What's going on..." he started.

"Sir, please step away and go about your business,"

demanded the officer.

Ricky then overheard the guards' radios squawk, "It happened on the twelfth floor, twelfth floor, code red. Shots were fired on the twelfth floor. Two officers down, proceed with caution."

Ricky obliged and turned toward the lobby doors. Just a hundred yards to go, he was so close. His feet wanted to run, but his mind warned him not to attract the attention of doing so. He slung the Steelers duffel over his shoulder and started the longest short walk of his life. One step, then two, and three. Four steps, five; his pace quickened and he was on his way. Less than a football field away was the exit, with only a defense of slot machines and drunk patrons to avoid.

But then a crowd of intoxicated cackling old ladies poured out right in front of Ricky when they exited the bar entrance to his right. His pace slowed to a shuffle as he frantically tried to find his way through or around them.

Elevator bay, 12th Floor
Caesar's Palace
★ 4:41 AM ★

The elevator door opened to reveal a middle-aged Asian business man. "What the hell . . ." he started saying when he noticed the bloodied nightmare about to join him inside. Before the man could even complete the sentence, Spider raised the gun to his face and emptied the chamber, sending a shower of red, spider-webbed cracks onto the mirror behind the man. Right as his elevator's doors closed, the adjacent elevator's doors opened just in time for one officer to catch a glimpse of Spider with a gun standing over a bloody lump of dead meat. "Code black, code black. Suspect in elevator two headed down," the guard spoke into the radio strapped to his shoulder.

Spider's luck continued to hold out.

Casino Floor
Caesar's Palace
★ 4:43 AM ★

Spider stepped out, blood draining from his head gash down his face and soaking his blue denim jacket to a shade of dark burgundy. His gun was drawn and his eyes were open wide and crazy. There was splatter and brain by-product all over the rest of his face and hair from the faceless, slumped corpse behind him.

A bystander awaiting elevators dove out of the way with an "oh fuck!" A woman attempted to sprint away, but her high heel had a different plan and snapped under her twisting body, dropping her instantly to the ground.

Spider turned right, ignoring the panicking people around him and looked right for the front doors. "RICKY!" he yelled at the top of his lungs. "Riiiiiickyyyyy!"

Ricky instinctively flinched but was so close to the door he just kept walking and didn't look back. An instant coldness engulfed him, like a demon of death had just possessed him. It was five more steps or a bullet in the back; that's what his whole life had come down to. He'd been fighting his demons for years, and he wasn't going to stop now. Just four more steps.

Spider squeezed the trigger and a bullet hit the chandelier far behind Ricky's head, sending down a shower of sharp crystal shrapnel that took out a group of guests like a devastating glass grenade.

Chaos ensued on the casino floor. People began running in every direction, screaming and crying. Gamblers and dealers alike hid under their tables, praying to go unnoticed. Flocks of chips went flying across the floor, but nobody bothered to pick them up; they were just running and hiding for their lives.

With just a few steps left, Ricky leaped and narrowly made it through the slight opening in the revolving door at Caesar's main entrance. Another round fired and this one was much closer, hitting the radius of the door opposite Ricky. Glass exploded to his left, and Ricky threw his hands up to cover his head from the shower of shards as he waited for the door to circle around and expose the opening.

Spider took off running toward the exit. Seconds later he got off another shot, then another, this time hitting a large woman, sending her bucket of slot machine coins flying in the air like a silver hailstorm crashing all over the marbled lobby floor.

Then there was another shot. But it didn't come from Spider's gun. It was from behind Spider. The group of security guards finally reappeared, running out of the opening elevator with weapons drawn. More security flooded in from the left and rear. A few guards took cover behind slot machines while others helped grab patrons and get them safely behind cover.

Ricky jumped down the front steps of Caesar's entrance and took off running into the parking structure next door.

Spider was on a terror. He put his shoulder down and crashed right through what was left of the half-shattered, now-stalled revolving door only to suddenly stop in his tracks. Pulling out just thirty feet in front of him was Ricky in a brand-new Mustang.

Ricky looked toward the door in shock to see the bloodied psychopath that used to be his friend standing so close to him. He watched Spider raise his gun. This was it; he thought he was home free, but Spider was too close.

Their eyes met in a translucent stare down. Ricky was close enough to feel the evil rage spewing from Spider's veins. He was close enough to smell the blood on his hands. He was close enough to see Spider's finger begin to squeeze the trigger.

Click, boom, click, boom!

All he could do was keep his foot on the gas and close his eyes. Ricky had never thought that bullets would hurt so little. Maybe it was the adrenaline running through his body, but he couldn't feel a thing. His foot lifted from the pedal.

When he opened his eyes, he saw Spider clearly. What he thought would be a painful final blur turned out to be the clearest vision he'd ever seen.

Spider's eyes still fixated on Ricky, but his gun dropped. His hands and arms followed. His body began to fold as he dropped to his knees.

Ricky looked Spider right in the eyes without a blink.

Click, boom, click, boom! Ricky flinched and came to his senses.

It wasn't from Spider's gun. It was from several guns behind Spider. The guards unloaded on him as Ricky watched red exit holes burst open through the front of his old friend's chest.

Click, boom!

One last shot sounded, and a new hole opened in Spider's face, right under his right eye. Spider fell to his face onto the marble steps of Caesar's Palace and his head burst into a mushy squash. The blood quickly filled the grooves and seams of the marble, which would forever leave a bloodstained memory map of the massacre.

The cops all huddled around Spider's corpse with guns still drawn. They were so consumed with the devastation that he'd caused and the chaos in the casino, that they never even noticed Ricky's car leaving the parking lot. Lots of cars were scurrying about and fleeing, so why was a red Mustang any different?

Ricky gathered himself and exited the parking area unscathed. He turned onto the strip toward The Flamingo Casino.

25

"Sunrise"

Rest Area Outside of Las Vegas
★ 5:51 AM ★

Ricky pulled to the far empty end of the rest area, near some massive Australian pine trees for cover. There was all but two cars and a lonely TaB soda semi occupying the whole park at this time of the morning. It was cold, but tolerable. Anything seemed tolerable at this point.

Ricky jiggled the keys and placed his hand upon the Mustang's trunk.

"You ready?" he said eagerly to the fiery redhead next to him.

"Yes!" replied Cinnamon nervously. He looked around the sleepy lot for one last attempt at caution. Thoughts raced through his head. *How much did Spider blow through at the casino? Was there enough for his daughter? Was there some left for Cinnamon? Did anyone follow him?* He opened the trunk wide and reached inside.

Ricky slid the old Steelers duffel closer toward himself, revealing a mustard-yellow briefcase underneath. It was the Bogey job! His body shivered, and for a second, he froze. After all the events over the last few hours, he completely forgot it was in there. After finding Bogey murdered, he realized that he never did anything with it. He had been so preoccupied with the Spider job that he must have just thrown it in the trunk with his clothes. He slid Spider's duffel aside and grabbed Bogey's briefcase handle.

"What's that?" asked Cinnamon.

"*That*, is a long story, but this could be our lucky day," said Ricky as he popped the brass latches open.

Their jaws dropped. Stacks of $100s silenced their every thought. Stacks upon stacks of cash neatly lined the case. Ricky quickly slammed it shut.

"Holy shit," he whispered under his breath.

"Oh my God," Cinnamon added. Ricky then snapped the trunk shut and turned to Cinnamon.

"Are you ready for a new life?"

"I sure as fuck am. What do we do now?" she eagerly replied.

Ricky took Cinnamon by the hand.

"We smoke the moment . . . how do you like Florida?"

SMOKE THE MOMENT

CHRIS 51